# KIDS CAN'T STOP READING
# THE CHOOSE YOUR
# OWN ADVENTURE® STORIES!

"I like Choose Your Own Adventure books because they're full of surprises. I can't wait to read more."

—Cary Romanos, age 12

"Makes you think thoroughly before making decisions."

—Hassan Stevenson, age 11

"I read five different stories in one night and that's a record for me. The different endings are fun."

—Timmy Sullivan, age 9

"It's great fun! I like the idea of making my own decisions."

—Anthony Ziccardi, age 11

## And teachers like this series, too:

"We have read and reread, worn thin, loved, loaned, bought for others, and donated to school libraries our Choose Your Own Adventure books."

## CHOOSE YOUR OWN ADVENTURE®— AND MAKE READING MORE FUN!

Bantam Books in the Choose Your Own Adventure® Series
Ask your bookseller for the books you have missed

Choose Your Own Adventure Books for younger readers

# GRAND CANYON ODYSSEY

## BY JAY LEIBOLD

ILLUSTRATED BY DON HEDIN

*An R.A. Montgomery Book*

BANTAM BOOKS

TORONTO • NEW YORK • LONDON • SYDNEY • AUCKLAND

RL 5, IL age 10 and up

GRAND CANYON ODYSSEY
*A Bantam Book / April 1985*

*CHOOSE YOUR OWN ADVENTURE*® *is a registered trademark
of Bantam Books, Inc.*
*Registered in U.S. Patent and Trademark Office and elsewhere.*

*Original conception of Edward Packard.*

ISBN 0-553-24822-7

*Published simultaneously in the United States and Canada*

Bantam Books are published by Bantam Books, Inc. Its trademark, consisting of the words "Bantam Books" and the por-
trayal of a rooster, is Registered in U.S. Patent and Trademark
Office and in other countries. Marca Registrada. Bantam
Books, Inc., 666 Fifth Avenue, New York, New York 10103.

PRINTED IN THE UNITED STATES OF AMERICA

O      0 9 8 7 6 5 4 3 2 1

**For my family**

# WARNING!!!

Do not read this book straight through from beginning to end! These pages contain many different adventures as you raft down the Colorado River in search of Bill Wilton's missing horses. Some of the adventures take place in the present, some in the past, and others in a completely different world. From time to time as you read along, you will be asked to make choices. Be careful—some choices are dangerous!

The adventures you have are the results of your choices. *You* are responsible because *you* choose! After you make a choice, follow the instructions to *see* what happens next.

Think carefully before you make a move. Any one choice could lead you to the horses or to exciting adventures—or to your doom.

Good Luck!

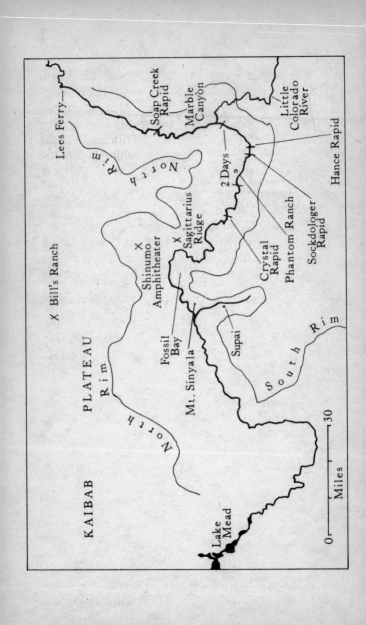

Two weeks ago a rancher named Bill Wilton called you with a mission. "My horses keep disappearing," he explained. "I've lost nearly three dozen head over the past few months. Our ranch is on the Kaibab Plateau, above the north rim of the Grand Canyon, and the strange thing is that the hoofprints just vanish at the edge of the canyon. We're completely baffled.

"I know your reputation as a river runner," he continued. "We want to hire you to float down the canyon and find the horses."

You did not hesitate to accept the job. "But," you told Bill, "It's an enormous place. I can't promise I'll find the horses. I'll do my best."

After Bill hung up, you called your friend Delia, a Navajo Indian who knows the secrets of the deserts and canyons of the Southwest. She agreed to be your guide. "I've always wanted to float through the Grand Canyon!" she said enthusiastically. "When do we leave?"

*Turn to page 2.*

"In two weeks," you replied. During those two weeks your anticipation has been building. You have run many rivers in the West, but never the greatest of them all—the Colorado as it cuts a mile-deep gorge through the Grand Canyon. It lies at the heart of the vast, mysterious region known as the Great American Desert, and most of it is still untracked.

Your fascination with the canyon began when you heard stories about time travel. It is said that just as the rock walls of the canyon are a reflection of the eons of geological time, certain travelers who descend into the gorge also descend into the corridors of time. Some say it is an infernal underworld; others say it is a place of vision.

*Turn to page 4.*

You jump into the river. When you come to the surface, you sense immediately that you are no longer in the canyon. Before you, the Colorado flows quietly, and there is open space all around. The tremendous roar of the river between the canyon walls is gone.

You look upriver. Something is coming down the middle of the channel. It's Delia in the raft!

"Delia!" you yell, waving your arms. "Here I am!"

Delia spots you, waves back, and rows over to you. You greet her happily and step into the raft. She takes it out into the current.

"Where have you been?" she asks.

"Oh, time traveling," you say casually. "What have you been up to?"

"You've missed out on a lot," Delia says. "I found the horses back in Middle Granite Gorge. Now we've nearly reached Lake Mead."

You are stunned. Lake Mead! That means you are at the end of the trip. You've gone forward in time! You are glad Delia found the horses, but you wish you'd been along for the adventure.

**The End**

**4**

Now, at Lees Ferry, you and Delia pack your supplies into the sixteen-foot rubber raft that will take you 277 miles down the river. You have food for four weeks, maps, rain gear, a two-way radio, and an air pump, all stowed in watertight bags. You check the oars and rowing frame, and make sure the raft is inflated to the correct pressure. Bill and the park ranger look on as the reddish brown river rushes by.

When everything is lashed tight into the raft, you and Delia go over your route with the ranger. A few miles from Lees Ferry you will enter Marble Canyon. It is two days to Upper Granite Gorge, then another two days and several treacherous rapids to Phantom Ranch. Once you pass Phantom Ranch you will head into the depths of the Middle Granite Gorge, where Bill suggests you look for the horses.

"Don't forget what our ranch brand looks like," Bill says. "It's the Lazy J-Bar-Z." He shows you a drawing of what to look for on the flanks of the horses.

At last all is ready. You and Delia put on your life jackets. Bill tips his hat and says, "Good luck." The ranger shakes your hands. You push the raft off the bank, hop in, and float into the current.

The river surges under your boat. It's good to be on the water with the sun hot overhead. The raft rocks gently, and you begin to settle into the rhythm of the river, ready to face the unknown.

*Turn to page 8.*

# 6

You grab a line coiled in the front of the boat and throw it to Delia, who is struggling to stay afloat in the foaming waves. The rope falls short of her outstretched arms, so you haul it in and throw it again.

In your rush to save Delia, you forget to navigate the rest of the rapid. The raft gets turned sideways and is flipped by a huge wave! You are flung into the water, and the boat is carried away from you.

*Turn to page 67.*

You look around. "Well, not exactly. But I know we are in the Grand Canyon of the Colorado River. Are you lost?"

"Me? Lost? Never! The Colorado River is exactly where I want to be." He pulls you toward him by your shirt. "You have heard of the Seven Golden Cities of Cibola?"

You shake your head.

A glint comes into his eyes. "They are made all of gold. Towers of gold and precious jewels glittering in the sun. Untold riches and glory. And I am nearly there! I can feel it!"

You try to step back, but he pulls harder on your shirt. "Do you know exactly where the Seven Golden Cities are?" he demands. "Tell me where they are!"

"I've never heard of them," you insist.

He releases you. "Then why not join me?" he offers. "Together we will find them and become rich and famous."

You consider Don Pizarro's offer. You have doubts about him, but it might be good to have a companion while you figure out how to get back to your own time. And who knows—maybe the Seven Golden Cities of Cibola really exist!

*If you say, "Yes, I will join you with pleasure,"*
*turn to page 76.*

*If you decline his offer, turn to page 97.*

In the late afternoon the walls of Marble Canyon begin to glow a rose color. You ask Delia if she thinks it is possible to travel through time in the canyon.

"I've never known anyone to do it," she replies. "But it may be possible. The canyon is a very powerful place. It is the navel of the universe, the place from which people emerged from a previous world. Many things are possible in a place so near to the source of life."

Delia pauses for a moment. "Coyote is known to frequent the canyon. He is a great trickster and practicer of sorcery. He can change himself into any shape."

Your conversation is interrupted by the roar of a large rapid downstream. "That must be Soap Creek," you say. "Should we run it?"

"It's awfully late in the day," Delia says. "Maybe we should wait till morning. On the other hand, it would feel good to get the first big rapid under our belts."

*If you want to run Soap Creek Rapid now,
turn to page 10.*

*If you decide to camp for the night,
turn to page 50.*

"The cliff!" you cry, and you and Delia leap onto the rock wall. Somehow you find handholds and rocket up the first ten feet of the cliff. The mountain lion springs, but you are just out of its reach. It paces back and forth below you, waiting for you to make a mistake.

You look at Delia. "I guess there's only one way to go," she says. You climb very carefully up the cliff, testing each handhold. You know you could never scale a wall this difficult if it weren't for the mountain lion. Your adrenaline comes to the rescue, and when you get to the top, it is too dark to go any farther. You and Delia decide to sleep.

When dawn breaks, you find you are on a broad plateau. And there is a herd of horses, right in front of you! You look for brands on their flanks. They are Bill's.

You and Delia look at each other and start laughing. "Thank goodness for the mountain lion," she says. "Otherwise, we never would have found the horses."

"But how did they get *here*?" you wonder out loud.

Delia shakes her head. "I imagine it will always be a mystery to us. Let's not question our good fortune."

"Okay," you agree. "Let's tell Bill. We can let him figure out how to get the horses out."

**The End**

You stop above Soap Creek Rapid to plan your line down it. The roar of the churning white water sends a thrill through your bones. You go back to the raft and head out into the rapid.

A tongue of smooth, fast water draws you in. You make sure your bow is pointed straight into the haystacks—enormous, frothing waves—waiting at the end of the tongue. You hit them head on. The boat rises steeply to the top of the first wave, then plunges down to crash into the next one. This one breaks over the bow with such force that it knocks you off your seat. When you recover the oars, you realize Delia is not in the boat!

You look for her frantically. When you spot her downriver, her arms are flailing as she struggles to stay afloat.

*If you try to pull Delia out by hand,
turn to page 24.*

*If you toss her a rope, turn to page 6.*

Although the prospect terrifies you, you agree to lead the expedition. "I think you are right— Powell would have wanted us to go on," you tell the crew.

You are terrified because you know how much is against you. The crew is small; your provisions are nearly gone; the boats are battered; and, most of all, the river before you is dangerous and unknown. This is not the same river you were floating down in your raft; it is the Colorado before the dams were built. It is even wilder and more unpredictable.

The odds are against you and nothing can make up for the loss of Powell. But if you make it you will be a hero. You walk down to the wooden boats and prepare to put into the river.

## The End

Much as you would like to stay with Powell and complete his famous expedition, you decide to try to return to your own time. Delia is probably wondering where you are—if she survived the rapid.

You quietly slip away from Powell and the crew gathered around the camp fire, put on your old clothes, and walk to the river. You take a deep breath and dive in.

*If you stay under for thirty seconds, turn to page 22.*

*If you stay under for sixty seconds, turn to page 18.*

"Quick!" you yell to Delia. "We've got to get to high ground. The flood water is coming!"

Delia runs to join you, and together you scramble up the slope. You can hear the roar of the water as it races closer and closer. You push yourself faster and nearly escape the flood crest—but not quite. The water picks you and Delia up at the waists and lifts you off the side of the canyon into the flood.

*Turn to page 21.*

"I can't do it," you tell the crew. "I can't take over. I'm not qualified."

They are disappointed but manage to convince someone to be captain, and you set off down the river. With your reduced numbers, you can all fit into one boat.

Although the first rapid you come to looks difficult, you think it can be run. The new captain disagrees. "Let's portage," he says.

"Wait a minute," you object. "I know it won't be easy, but I think we can run it. The channel is so narrow here that it would be more dangerous to portage than to run it."

The captain gives you a cold stare. "Are you making the decisions or am I?"

You must give in. He is the captain and has the right to decide, so you pull the boat up on the bank for portage. As you begin to let it down the rapid by rope, your worst fears come true. The crew can't hold the boat in the narrow channel and strong current. They must either let go of the ropes or be dragged into the rapids themselves.

They let go. The boat, along with your supplies, is swept away by the white torrent. You are left stranded and helpless in the Grand Canyon.

**The End**

You decline Powell's invitation, and no one else on the crew will go with him. "All right, then," he says. "I'll go by myself."

As soon as he is out of earshot, some of the crew members start grumbling. A man named Howland says, "This expedition is doomed. We're living on nothing but musty flour and coffee. The rest of our rations have been spoiled or lost in the river. We have only one tattered blanket apiece and no protection from the rain. One boat has already been smashed on the rocks, and just listen to the roar of the rapids below us! This trip will never end."

"We could climb out a side canyon," another adds. "We can hike up to the plateau and find the Mormon settlement up there. I think it's our only chance."

Howland leans over and whispers confidentially to you, "Major Powell is a great explorer and geologist. But I think he's a little crazy in the head. This canyon can do it to you. We'll all go crazy if starvation or rapids don't kill us first."

Another crewman declares he will leave the expedition, too. The three of them look at you expectantly.

---

*If you join them and abandon the expedition, turn to page 38.*

*If you decide to stay with Powell, turn to page 20.*

"I'll get help from camp," you call to Powell.

"Hurry!" he gasps.

You run along the bench and luckily find an easier way down to camp. You arrive breathless and tell the crew, "Come help quick! Major Powell is stuck on a cliff!"

The crew rushes to follow you back up to the high bench. Powell lies at the foot of the cliff he was on. You climb down to his body, but you are too late.

You make your way back to camp, feeling terrible. No one says anything.

The next morning four members of the crew approach you. "Three of the men have left the expedition," one of them tells you. "They're trying to hike out a side canyon. The rest of us have decided to carry on. We think Powell would want that. And we want you to be the captain."

*If you accept leadership of the expedition, turn to page 11.*

*If you decline, turn to page 14.*

The chance to join Powell for the rest of the expedition is too good to pass up. You just hope Delia survived the rapid. If she did, you know she will be able to take care of herself.

The rest of the trip is glorious. You have never been on a river so wild and untamed. This is the Colorado before the dams were built. There are several hair-raising rapids and some difficult portages, in which you have to let the boats down over rapids by ropes. But you make it through the canyon just as your provisions give out. You enter the flat water at the end of the canyon, where you find a Mormon settlement.

You return to great acclaim in Washington, D.C. You like running uncharted rivers so much you decide you don't want to go back to your own time. The rest of your days are spent exploring the rivers of the West and writing accounts of your expeditions.

**The End**

# 18

You fight your way to the surface of the river, swim to the bank, and pass out. When you come to, it is broad daylight. There are footprints in the sand in front of you.

You get up and follow the footprints. Suddenly a voice demands, "Who are you?"

You look up. Before you stands a man with a black mustache, black pointed beard, and fierce-looking eyes. His chest and arms are encased in shiny silver armor. He wears a plumed helmet and carries a sword in his hand.

You can't help but blurt out, "Who are *you?*"

"Signor Don Pizarro de Manquila." He throws out his chest and adds proudly, "I am a conquistador!"

You gape at him. If he is a conquistador, you are in the sixteenth century!

His voice becomes soft as he inquires, "Would you, perhaps, know where we are?"

*Turn to page 7.*

"Count me out," you say to Howland. "I'm staying with Major Powell."

"It's your life," Howland says, shrugging. He cannot get anyone else to join him and the other two deserters.

The next morning the deserters leave for the rim of the canyon. To your surprise, Powell does not try to stop them. "To tell you the truth," he confides to you, "I'm not sure it's such a bad idea. I almost decided to do the same. I don't know what our chances are of getting out alive. But we've come this far—we can't give up now."

Powell's words make you think twice about staying with him. After a skimpy meal of musty flour cakes and coffee, you decide to slip away to the river. Since it brought you here, perhaps it can take you back to your own time.

No one notices you leave after breakfast. You go down to the water, switch clothes, and stand on the bank of the river.

*Turn to page 3.*

You and Delia try to hold on to each other, but the swirling currents of the flood separate you. You are carried downriver in the fast-moving water and watch, helpless, as Delia is carried farther and farther away.

Fighting to keep your head above the surface of the water, you look around to get a sense of where the flood is taking you. To your left, about a quarter of a mile away, you spot dry land. Should you try to swim to it, or should you let the flood take you where it will?

*If you swim for dry land, turn to page 30.*

*If you decide to let the current carry you, turn to page 105.*

You stay under the water for thirty seconds, then come back up and swim to shore. There, beside a roaring breakfast fire, is Delia!

"Where have you been?" she asks.

"I—I—" you sputter. "I've been traveling in time."

She raises her eyebrows. "You'll have to tell me about it. But right now we have work to do. While you've been traveling in time, I managed to survive the rapid and keep going down the river. We're in the Middle Granite Gorge now, and it's time to start looking for the horses." She spreads out a map, and you look at it with her.

"The way I see it," Delia says, "we have two choices. We could either go to the top of the Sagittarius Ridge to get a view of the area, or we could go into the huge Shinumo Amphitheater."

*If you decide to go into Shinumo Amphitheater, turn to page 69.*

*If you want to climb Sagittarius Ridge, turn to page 66.*

You pull hard on the oars to get to Delia, but the river pushes her just out of your reach. With one last heave, you finally come close enough to thrust out your hand. She grabs it and pulls herself in. You both lie gasping as the raft moves into quiet waters. You have survived the river's first test and decide to make camp on a sandy beach.

The next two days as you head on down the canyon into Upper Granite Gorge are uneventful.

At dusk of the second day, just after you have set up camp, a call comes through on the radio.

*Turn to page 57.*

You gulp down Delia's herb mixture. To your surprise, it tastes good. You grow drowsy and fall asleep.

When you wake up, the fang marks on your arm have started to heal. Delia smiles as you sit up. "It's an old remedy. It has never failed."

You continue up into the amphitheater. Late in the day Delia stops you to point out one of the cliffs that rings the amphitheater. A huge honeycomb of square rooms is backed up against the rock wall. The mud of the structure blends in perfectly with the rock behind it so that it seems to be growing out of the wall.

"It's a cliff dwelling," Delia says. "It was built long ago by the Pueblos. But I didn't know one was in this spot." You hike up to take a look. Delia goes inside while you look at ancient pictographs carved on the rock behind the cliff dwelling.

"It looks as if someone still lives here," Delia calls from inside.

*Turn to page 56.*

It takes you two hours to fix the raft. The rain continues to come down in sheets. When you finish the job, you get back on the water.

That night you are dunked three more times by unseen rocks and waves. Sunrise finds you exhausted and chilled. You feel better when the rain stops, but a look at the map shows that you lost too much time during the night.

"We'll never make it to Phantom Ranch before the flood," you say. "The big rapids are still ahead of us."

"We'll just have to find a way to hike out," Delia says, scanning the cliffs on your right.

You land on shore and pull the raft out of the water. Delia checks out a side canyon while you climb up to a bench two hundred feet above the river. From there you can see no route to the rim, so you start back down to the raft where Delia is now waiting. On your way you glance up the canyon and gasp at what you see.

A wall of water is rolling down the canyon like a huge moving mountain. You have never seen anything like it. The flood crest will reach you in a matter of minutes. You must act quickly!

*Turn to page 13.*

Your long johns are the one thing that could reach Powell. You slip them off, lie on your stomach, and dangle them as far down as you can.

"Can you grab these?" you call to Powell.

He grunts, then says, "I think I can reach them. I'll try." Suddenly there is a great weight on your arm. You pull as hard as you dare without ripping the long johns. Powell grunts again, then calls, "I can make it the rest of the way myself."

You stand up and pull your long johns and pants back on. Soon Powell appears with a bemused look on his face. "I always seem to be getting myself into trouble," he says. Then he adds, "I'm glad you changed clothes."

Powell makes his observations, carefully noting the flora, fauna, types of rock, and contour of the land. Then the two of you find an easier way back to camp.

That night, after an unsatisfying dinner of musty flour cakes and coffee, you start to think about trying to get back to your own time. Perhaps you could do it by diving back into the river. Your river-running friends will say you are crazy to give up the chance to finish Powell's expedition with him, but you also know Bill is counting on you.

*If you try to get back to your own time by diving into the river again, turn to page 12.*

*If you stay with Powell, turn to page 17.*

"I think we can make it in the raft," you tell the ranger. "If worse comes to worst, we'll call for help on the radio."

"Roger," the ranger says. "Good luck, and keep us posted on your position."

You repack the raft and get back on the river immediately. Night falls quickly, and an eerie darkness descends over the river. Bats swoop low over the water, their wings fluttering near your heads. It is difficult to see, and you must rely almost entirely on your sense of hearing. To make things worse, the storm the ranger predicted arrives.

"It's too bad we can't do what my ancestors did when the Great Flood came," Delia comments. "They turned themselves into fish, so they wouldn't drown. Some Indians still will not eat fish for fear of eating an ancestor."

Suddenly a boulder appears right in front of you. You have no time to avoid it. The raft crashes into it head-on, and you and Delia are thrown out. Luckily, you both manage to grab hold of the boat and kick to shore. You pull it up on the beach and sit in the rain, wondering what can go wrong next.

*Turn to page 37.*

In the surging flood currents, you swim with strong strokes for dry land. You soon discover it is hard just to keep your head above water, much less swim anywhere. When you think your strength is all gone, a friendly current comes along and carries you to the shore. Exhausted, you lie on the beach, unable to move.

A voice rouses you. "So there you are!"

You open your eyes. "Delia!" you cry. "You made it to shore!"

"With luck," she says. "After the flood carried me off, I found the raft floating upside down. The oars and all our supplies were gone, but I grabbed it and guided it here."

"I wonder where we are."

"It's some sort of island," she replies. "I've walked around it. We're completely surrounded by water."

"So we can't make it to the rim from here," you say.

"No," she replies, eyeing the land in the distance. "But we could get back in the water after we rest."

*Go on to the next page.*

You look at the swift, silty water going by. "We probably shouldn't stay here too long. But we don't have any oars, and that flood water looks unpredictable."

"We could stay here for the night," Delia suggests. "Maybe by morning the water will have receded."

*If you get back in the water, turn to page 45.*

*If you wait for the water to recede, go on to the next page.*

"Let's stay here until the water goes down," you decide. "It looks too fast right now."

You make a comfortable shelter of pine boughs and dine on roots and berries around the campfire. You sleep well that night, tired by the day's events.

The next morning you wake to find the water has receded and left you stranded! The "island" is really a plateau, a flattop ringed by an impassable five-hundred-foot drop. "I should have known," Delia says.

But this is only the first shock of the day. You explore the plateau and find it is inhabited by miniature dinosaurs, the size of lizards!

*Turn to page 49.*

Delia looks at the map for a while, then says, "It won't be easy, but I've found a route up to the north rim and Kaibab Plateau."

"Let's go," you say. You pack food, water, and the map and start the long, upward climb to the rim of the canyon. The rain makes the loose dirt of the canyon slopes slippery, and you must feel your way in the dark. After four hours of hard climbing, you pause for a rest. You are high enough to feel safe from the flood, and soon you and Delia fall asleep under the protection of a tree.

Delia wakes in the first light of dawn. The rain has stopped. "Listen!" she says. "What's that?"

A rumbling, like the sound of distant thunder, is coming from the other side of the ridge to your right.

*If you investigate the rumbling, turn to page 48.*

*If you push on toward the rim, turn to page 40.*

"Let's round up the horses and ride out," you say. "It may be impossible to find this place again."

You each ride a horse bareback. Delia finds a faint trail traversing the wall of the amphitheater and leads the horses up the narrow path single file. You bring up the rear.

After a hot climb, you reach the rim. The pines and meadows of the Kaibab Plateau spread out before you.

"The trail ends here," Delia says. "I wonder who could have made it?"

Just then you see a rider approaching from the distance. He gallops toward you at high speed. You wonder if he is friendly.

*If you take the horses and gallop away from him, turn to page 53.*

*If you wait for the rider to arrive, turn to page 39.*

"I don't know what's out there," you say to Delia as you come back to the campfire, "but I don't think I want to find out."

The yellow eyes do not appear again that night. The next morning you make a perfect run of Soap Creek Rapid and head on down the river. It takes three days to get to Phantom Ranch. During that time you make successful runs of some of the most-feared rapids of the river. Finally you enter Middle Granite Gorge, the most remote part of the canyon. Immense walls of granite soar above you.

Before you can look for the horses, you must face Crystal Rapid. River runners rate it a ten, making it the most difficult possible. You pull up to survey it from a rock overlooking the rapid.

Crystal is a narrow chute filled with rocks, whirlpools, and a huge depression in the water. "If we can make a quick turn around that first rock," you suggest, "then we can shoot past the next rock and down the channel between the whirlpool and the hole."

*Turn to page 47.*

"Listen," Delia says. "What's that hissing?"

It's the unmistakable sound of air escaping from the raft. "The boulder ripped a hole in the boat," you say. "That does it. I'm calling for a helicopter. It can't be any worse than this."

You switch on the radio, but nothing happens. You look at Delia. "It must have been broken in the crash," you say.

"We'll have to patch the raft. Or," she suggests, "we could hike out from here. I bet we could find a side canyon that would lead up to the rim."

*If you patch the raft, turn to page 26.*

*If you look for a side canyon, turn to page 34.*

"I'm in. I'll go with you," you say to Howland. "The expedition sounds hopeless."

He looks at the rest of the crew, but they decide to stay. "Have it your way," he says to them. "We'll send in a search party for you."

Howland waits until morning to announce his intentions to Powell. To your surprise, Powell does not try to stop you. He offers the four of you some provisions for the trip, but Howland refuses, saying, "I've got my rifle. We'll find some game on the plateau."

Powell gives you a duplicate set of trip journals and a letter for his family. He wishes you luck, and you set off with Howland up a side canyon for the rim.

You are never heard from again.

**The End**

You wait for the horseman to arrive. Soon you are face to face. He has a long black mustache, and his eyes are narrowed in anger.

"Where'd you get them horses?" he demands.

"None of your business," you say. "They belong to Bill Wilton."

"They belong to me," the man snarls as he whips a rifle out of his saddle. "See, we rustle horses. And it's too bad for you that you found them because that means you're going to come back to our hideout with me." He motions with the rifle. "Now get moving."

The rustler makes Delia lead the herd while you bring up the rear with him. He keeps his rifle on you the whole time and warns Delia not to try to escape.

But something else is going on, too. The horses are becoming uneasy. Delia glances back, and you can tell she notices it also. The horses are growing more and more restless by the minute. Maybe this is your chance to escape.

*If you whoop and holler to try to get the horses to stampede, turn to page 51.*

*If you try to distract the rustler by saying, "Watch out for that rattlesnake!" turn to page 44.*

You don't like the sound of the rumbling. "Let's keep going up to the rim," you say.

You push on up. Soon you see several places ahead where landslides block your path.

"That must have been what caused the rumbling," Delia says.

"Yes," you agree. "But now where do we go?"

Delia just starts to answer when a loud crack splits the air above you. You look up in time to see a mass of soil and rock break off from the hillside. It quickly gathers momentum. Before you have time to take a step, you are buried under tons of rock and dirt.

**The End**

You miss the rock, but the hole is waiting for you. The raft plunges into it. Water crashes over your head, and for a few terrifying seconds you feel its weight smother you. But then the hole spits you out the other end. You are still afloat, though swamped. Delia bails furiously while you navigate the rest of the rapid. When you make it into calm water, you breathe a long sigh of relief.

You pull up on shore and camp for the night. Now you can start looking for the horses. In the morning Delia consults the map over breakfast.

"I see two good possibilities from here," she says. "We could go into Shinumo Amphitheater, which is an enormous walled-in valley, or we could climb up to Sagittarius Ridge, where we might have a view."

*If you explore Shinumo Amphitheater, turn to page 69.*

*If you climb Sagittarius Ridge, turn to page 66.*

"Let's walk out," you decide. "I think it's too dangerous to ride."

You find a way out of the amphitheater and up to the north rim and Kaibab Plateau. After three long, hot days of hiking you reach the ranger station, nearly dead of heat and thirst.

The ranger greets you warmly. "Thank goodness you escaped the flood!" he says. "We had almost given up hope."

"And we found some of the horses, too," you say.

"Splendid! That was the only remaining mystery," he says. "Just last night Bill Wilton caught a couple of rustlers on his ranch. We found a lot of his horses at their hideout."

"Rustlers!" you exclaim. "So that's what's been happening to the horses."

"Yes. The rustlers confessed to it all. The only thing we couldn't get out of them was where they were hiding the rest of the horses. But now you've provided the last piece in the puzzle."

**The End**

"Watch out for that rattlesnake!" you cry. The rustler lets out a yelp and looks all around for the snake. You dig your heels into your horse, hoping to escape in the confusion. Delia picks up your cue and does the same.

It takes the rustler a moment to figure out what you are doing, but he recovers quickly. He is a sharpshooter. Even at long range, he needs only one shot apiece to bring you and Delia down.

**The End**

You take a rest, then board the raft and get back into the swift water. You hope you can navigate to the canyon wall and walk out from there.

A large brown object is swirling in an eddy ahead of you. "What's that?" you ask. "It looks like a log."

You move closer and find it is not a log at all. It is a horse floating in the river, its brown tail trailing behind.

"It's dead," Delia says. "The flood must have gotten it."

You take a closer look. The Lazy J-Bar-Z is clearly branded on the horse's flank.

You go on downstream and find many more dead horses. It is a terrible sight. You'll have some bad news for Bill when you make it out of the canyon.

**The End**

You step back from the gates of the city. "All right, Don Pizarro," you say. "The gold is yours." You leave him to his riches and head back toward the river. You hope it can return you to your own time.

A day of hiking brings you to its banks. You gaze down at the brown current flowing by.

*Turn to page 3*.

Delia agrees with you, and the two of you go back to the raft. The roar of the rapid below sends the blood pounding in your ears. The water seems to disappear over the lip of the rapid into nothingness. The rapid swiftly sucks you in. Waves crash over the bow and throw the boat around as you make your turn around the first rock. But then the raft is pitched up nearly vertically on a wave, and you lose sight of your course for a moment. You come over the top of the wave to find you are headed straight for the second rock! You must avoid it, but the choices are harrowing: to your right is a seething whirlpool, and to your left is the hole.

*If you go to your right, turn to page 55.*

*If you go to your left, turn to page 42.*

You climb over the ridge to investigate the rumbling and find yourself in a big rock amphitheater.

"Listen," Delia says again.

There is silence. You look at her.

"Let's keep going," she says.

You walk into the amphitheater. A rhythmic thumping starts close by.

"Hoofbeats!" you exclaim. "So that's what the rumbling was. They're coming from the other side of those pines."

You run through the pines and stop abruptly. There, in front of you, is a herd of horses, manes blowing in the wind, nostrils flaring.

You walk into the herd. "These are some of Bill's, all right," you say. "They've got the Lazy J-Bar-Z brand. I wonder what they're doing here?"

"The real question is, how do we get them out of here?" Delia asks.

---

*If you try to ride out and bring the horses with you, turn to page 35.*

*If you decide to walk out and report to Bill, turn to page 43.*

"Fascinating," Delia says. "For years scientists have speculated about the possibility of evolution progressing differently on a plateau such as this. This place has been separated from the main body of the Kaibab Plateau for millions of years. The plants and animals have evolved separately from those of the mainland. What a discovery!"

"But how are we going to tell the world about it?" you ask. "I sure hope they send a search plane for us soon."

"I don't know about you," Delia replies, "but I'd be just as happy to stay here. We have plenty of food and shelter. I'd like to study the dinosaurs. If we tell the world about them, they'll just turn this plateau into a tourist attraction."

You realize that Delia is right. You resign yourself to life with the dinosaurs on what you and she name Evolution Plateau.

**The End**

# 50

You save Soap Creek Rapid for morning and camp for the night in a shady grove by the river. As you sit by the campfire, you ask Delia to tell you more legends about the Grand Canyon.

"The Little Horses are supposed to live here," she says. "Long ago they got trapped in the canyon and developed separately from the rest of their species. They are half the size of normal horses and are too wild to be tamed. I hear they are also very clever."

Suddenly you see something flash behind Delia. "What's that?" you wonder aloud.

She turns around. "I didn't see anything."

"There's something out there," you say, getting up. "I'm going to take a look." You walk to the edge of the firelight. In the darkness beyond the campfire, two bright yellow eyes are blinking at you. There is something magnetic about them. They are luring you out into the night. You wonder if you should follow them.

*If you follow the yellow eyes, turn to page 72.*

*If you resist the lure and return to the campfire, turn to page 36.*

You let out a loud whoop. Delia catches on immediately and lets loose a string of Navajo war yells.

"Hey!" the rustler says. "What's going on? Cut that out!" But he can't figure out what you're up to.

Your whoops and hollers reach a crescendo that excites the horses to the breaking point. In a great rumble of hoofbeats, they stampede.

"Let's go!" you yell. You and Delia dig your heels into your horses and take off. The surprised rustler is caught in the stampede, knocked off his horse, and trampled by the herd.

After the horses have calmed down, you and Delia gather them up and gallop off to Bill Wilton's ranch.

## The End

You decide you don't want to confront the lone rider. "Let's go!" you yell. "Giddyap!"

You, Delia, and the horses race across a sage-brush clearing. The horseman comes after you.

"He's catching up!" Delia cries. You urge your horses on.

But his horse is faster. He pulls closer and closer. You look back to see him right behind you, whirling a lasso, his teeth bared. He aims the lasso for your head. You grab it in midair and give it a jerk. He is pulled off his horse and left face down in the dust. You gather the horses together and gallop toward Bill Wilton's ranch.

### The End

"The horses must be destined for Uqbar," you say. "How else can anyone explain the coincidence of the Lazy J-Bar-Z and the pictograph?"

"That's what we decided," Amanda says. "But if the horses want to return, they are free to go."

"Fine," you say.

You stay the night at Uqbar. In the morning you say goodbye to Amanda and wish her luck with the community. "We won't tell anyone about it," you promise.

You and Delia break camp and head back to the raft. "What will we tell Bill?" Delia asks.

"I'm not sure," you say. "We'll have to assume the horses will return when they are ready."

## The End

Hoping your momentum will carry you through the whirlpool, you move to your right to avoid the rock.

The raft grazes the rock, and the impact spins you around in a half circle. Suddenly you are going backward into the whirlpool!

You try desperately to row away from it, but it sucks you in and spins you around at dizzying speed. You try with all your strength to row out, but the current has you in its grip. Finally you must give up. The whirlpool swallows you whole.

**The End**

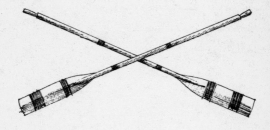

You start to join her when one of the pictographs catches your eye. "Delia! Come here," you cry. "The Lazy J-Bar-Z is etched on the wall!"

Delia comes out and examines the pictograph. "How strange!" she exclaims.

"Should we go inside and explore?" you ask.

"We could do that," she answers. "Or we could make camp up around the bend. From there we could see if anyone approaches."

*If you go inside, turn to page 65.*

*If you make camp around the bend, turn to page 58.*

"There's bad news," the ranger's voice crackles. "A big storm is coming your way, and you've got to get out of there fast. It's been raining heavily in the Rockies, and flood waters are moving down the river at high speed. Several people have already died in flash floods in Utah. We estimate the flood crest will reach the canyon in twenty-four hours. You've got to be out by then or you'll drown."

"Where should we come out?" you ask.

"It would be best if you could get back on the river tonight and go down to Phantom Ranch," he replies. "You can walk out on the trail from there." He pauses. "If you don't think you can make it, we can try a helicopter rescue, but that would be even more risky at night in the storm."

*If you say, "Let's not risk any more lives than necessary; we'll come out in the raft,"*
*turn to page 29.*

*If you ask for a helicopter rescue,*
*turn to page 96.*

# 58

You decide to make camp. At first you don't see anyone, but then, in the last light of day, you spot something moving toward you up the valley.

"Can you see what it is?" you whisper.

Delia peers into the dim light. "It's a girl with a horse," she says.

"A horse!" you say. "Let's find out who she is."

The girl pauses at the entrance to the cliff dwelling. You both run down. She is startled, but collects herself enough to ask, "What do you want?"

"We're looking for some lost horses," you say.

She eyes you for a moment. "Come inside," she says. You and Delia follow her into the cliff house. She leads you through many rooms and hallways until you arrive in a large torchlit room. It is full of kids busily preparing their evening meal.

*Turn to page 60.*

Turn to page 69.

"My name is Amanda," she says to you. "Our community is called Uqbar. We have all run away from home for one reason or another. We work together here, growing our own food and making things for ourselves. Please don't tell anyone about us. We're happy here, away from the adult world."

"What about the horses?" you ask.

"We have a whole herd," Amanda says. "We don't know where they come from. But we have noticed they have the same marking on their flanks as a pictograph outside."

"And that marking is also the brand for Bill Wilton's ranch!" you say. "I don't know what to make of this."

"The horses must have been attracted by the pictograph for some reason," Delia says. "Perhaps they belong here."

*If you think the horses are destined to stay in Uqbar, turn to page 54.*

*If you try to take them back to Bill, turn to page 77.*

The herb mixture looks awful. "I don't think I can drink it," you say to Delia.

"Why not?" she asks.

You think quickly. "Um—I'm allergic to some of the things in it. We'd better go back to camp and get the snakebite kit."

You head down, even though you know it is not a good idea to move after a rattlesnake bite because walking speeds the flow of the venom through your system.

The heat of the day makes the venom move even faster. The bite on your arm swells. Soon you feel dizzy. You have only made it halfway back when you collapse, and there is nothing Delia can do to save you.

**The End**

"I'll go up the cliffs with you," you say to Powell. "Good," he says. "Why don't you lead?"

The climb alternates between sections of vertical cliff and flat benches. Luckily, your previous rock-climbing experience has prepared you for this.

You pull yourself up over an especially difficult section and wait for Powell to catch up. But he doesn't appear, and a few moments later he calls, "I'm stuck! I can't move up or down."

You lean out over the edge of the cliff and see him seven feet below, clinging to the face of the rock. You realize that the last difficult move you made on the cliff is impossible for Powell because he has only one arm.

"I can't hold on much longer," he cries. "Do something quickly!"

*If you run back to camp to get help, turn to page 16.*

*If you take off your long johns and try to pull him up with them, turn to page 27.*

You run to where you last saw the eyes. They seem to have disappeared. Then, over to your left—there they are, waiting patiently.

The eyes continue to lead you on. You cling to the narrow ledge as the slope gets steeper. At one point you must crawl through a rock tunnel in the hillside, and when you come out on the other side, you follow the eyes up a narrow side canyon to a small rocky nook in the cliffs. A long, tall entrance in the rock leads into a passage with granite walls close on either side. The eyes take you inside. They seem to know where to go.

*Turn to page 78.*

"Let's take a look inside," you say.

You and Delia remove your packs and enter the cliff dwelling. It is quiet inside, and you neither see nor hear anyone else.

The place is huge. Each room leads on to another or to a room above by way of a ladder. You climb into room after room littered with tools, wooden beams, and clay bricks, until you come out on the flattop of the cliff dwelling. Behind you is the rock wall of the amphitheater and in front of you the ridges of the Grand Canyon stretch into the distance.

Something growls behind you. You turn quickly. A mountain lion, ten feet away, is crouched to attack!

*If you scale the rock wall to escape,
turn to page 9.*

*If you run back down the ladder into the cliff
dwelling, turn to page 71.*

You and Delia set out for Sagittarius Ridge with plenty of food and water in your packs. You see no sign of the horses as you climb the steep, slippery slopes of the ridge. By the time you make it to the top, it is late in the day. You have a snack and take in the view.

With no warning, storm clouds appear in the west. The wind picks up, the clouds come rolling in, and big drops of rain start to fall as lightning cracks the sky.

"We'd better get off the ridge fast," Delia says.

You start down quickly. Static electricity buzzes all around you. You move as fast as you can on the slippery rocks, but you are not fast enough. In a split second, a bolt of lightning strikes, leaving only your ashes.

**The End**

You flounder in the water, trying to get to shore. Gasping, you finally manage to pull yourself onto a sandy beach. You are wet and your head hurts, but otherwise you are all right. You get to your feet and scan the river for Delia.

A voice behind you barks, "Quit playing in the water and help unload the boats!"

You whirl around. Before you stands a man with a bushy brown beard and penetrating gray eyes. He has only one arm. You immediately recognize him from your knowledge of river lore.

"Major Powell!" you cry in astonishment.

He raises his eyebrows. "That's my name. You look as if you've seen a ghost." He looks you over. "And put on some decent clothes. Where did you get that strange outfit?"

*Turn to page 75.*

Continue reading. To take a different path, turn to page 41.

"Let's try Shinumo Amphitheater," you say.

Delia agrees, and you load your packs and set off. Late in the morning you stop for a breather under a tree. You casually stretch out your arm to lean against a branch—without realizing a rattlesnake is lounging there. Its bite is lightning quick. You sink to the ground holding your arm.

Delia makes a cut across each fang mark and squeezes out the venom. "I forgot the snakebite kit," you moan. You feel weak and feverish.

"Keep still," Delia says. "I will prepare a cure."

She gathers herbs, roots, and other things you can't see and stirs them all together. She hands the concoction to you, and you look at it, feeling doubtful about drinking the strange mixture.

*If you drink the herb mixture, turn to page 25.*

*If you say you'd rather go back to camp for the snakebite kit, turn to page 61.*

"Oh no, you don't!" you tell Don Pizarro. "We're partners."

He bares his teeth and hisses, "It's all mine!"

You grab his sword by the hilt and disarm him before he can swing it at you. He has a sudden change of mind. "Well," he says, sighing, "come on in."

You walk through the gates of the gleaming city, abandoned by its builders long ago. You marvel at the shining towers and the streets of gold.

"It's magnificent!" Don Pizarro announces to you. "But just imagine what the rest of the cities must look like. You stand guard here, and I'll go claim the others!" He hurries off in search of the remaining six cities of Cibola.

*Turn to page 114.*

You and Delia dash back to the ladder. You don't bother with the rungs; you just slide straight down them into the cliff dwelling.

But the mountain lion is even faster than you. It leaps from the roof into the cliff dwelling in a single bound—and in one more has you in its jaws.

**The End**

Whoever or whatever the yellow eyes belong to, they want to lead you somewhere. You can't resist their lure.

They disappear and reappear twenty feet ahead, waiting for you. Just as you are about to overtake them, they disappear and go farther. In this way the eyes lead you up a steep slope. The night grows darker.

You follow the eyes along a narrow ledge on the slope. Suddenly you don't know where you are, and you're not sure in which direction camp is. You stop and look back. Deep silence and darkness surround you. Panic takes hold. You look ahead for the yellow eyes. They are gone!

*If you run ahead to where you last saw the eyes, turn to page 63.*

*If you try to run back the way you came, turn to page 91.*

"I wouldn't want to take the horses away from their ancestors," you say to Coyote. "Thank you for showing them to me."

"If you follow the stream in front of you," Coyote replies, "you will find a trail. It will take you back to your camp."

Before you can say anything, Coyote bounds off. You head back to camp, eager to tell Delia about the events of the night. You're glad the horses have found their home, but you wonder what you will tell Bill when you get back.

## The End

You feel as if *you* are the ghost. Major John Wesley Powell, the famous explorer and geologist, was the first to attempt passage of the Grand Canyon in his legendary expedition of 1869. The river must have carried you back to the time of his expedition!

Powell is still watching you, so you set to work unloading the three battered wood expedition boats. Then you manage to find a pair of long johns and wool pants to wear. After you have helped set up camp, Powell points to a series of steep cliffs above you.

"I'm going up there to make some observations," he says to you. "How about coming along?"

You would like to accompany the famous river runner. But you are exhausted from the strange events of the day, and the cliffs look forbidding.

*If you say you'll go with Powell, turn to page 62.*

*If you stay in camp, turn to page 15.*

"I will join you," you say to Don Pizarro.

"Good," he says, clapping his hand on your shoulder. He points down the river. "We will go this way. I am certain it is not far." He strides ahead, armor clinking, and you follow.

Two hours of hiking in the hot sun brings you into a wide valley with gentle slopes. You come across a series of well-used paths. Farther up the valley you spot the mud walls of the dwellings of an Indian tribe.

"This must be where Pueblo Indians live," you say. "Maybe we should ask them if they know where the cities are."

"The natives are no help," Don Pizarro replies irritably. "I've tried to get information from them. They tell you nothing."

*Turn to page 82.*

"The horses may have come here by themselves," you say. "But I think we should return them to Bill."

"You are free to take them," Amanda replies. "If they return to us, then we'll know for sure they want to be here."

"Fair enough," you agree.

"We have a secret trail that leads out of the amphitheater," Amanda says. "I will show you where it is. It is a long, hard trip, but not impossible. You can take the horses out that way."

You leave at dawn the next morning. Amanda wishes you luck as you and Delia each mount one of the horses to lead the rest of the herd out. Bill will be happy to see them.

**The End**

You follow the eyes through the passage, winding to the right, then to the left. You stop for a moment and realize you are in a labyrinth. Your own eyes adjust, and you notice light is filtering in from somewhere above. You wonder if it is daybreak already. You hurry ahead, hoping that in the weak light you may be able to see the owner of the eyes.

But nothing is there. You have another moment of panic, but then you hear the soft pad of footsteps around the corner. You follow quickly, but every time you round a corner, the footsteps have just turned the next one.

Suddenly a small voice from behind you taunts, "Hey, you! Where are you going? You need some help?"

You turn, but see no one. The footsteps keep moving ahead.

*If you hurry to catch up with the footsteps,
turn to page 93.*

*If you stop to see who is talking to you,
turn to page 85.*

"You are a river," you answer.

"So I am," the gila monster says, amused. Suddenly a torrent of water comes down the passageway, picks you up, and carries you out of the labyrinth into a steep gulch. You fight your way out of the water and up onto dry ground. The gila monster once again stands in front of you.

"Now you have to answer my question," you remind him.

"Okay," he says, sighing. "What is it?"

"Where are the horses?"

"Ah, yes! The horses," he says. "They have joined their ancestors, the Little Horses, in a pasture in the canyon. No human will ever find them. Now, if you walk down this gulch you will find your camp." He scampers under a rock and disappears.

You head back to camp with a lot of questions for Delia about gila monsters.

**The End**

"You are a cave," you answer.

The gila monster breaks out in demonic laughter.

"What's wrong with my answer?" you demand.

He keeps laughing, then finally says, "Your answer is not so bad. But it's not the one I wanted. Perhaps I will give you a second chance. Answer this one: the more of me you take away, the larger I grow. What am I?"

---

*If you say, "I'm tired of this, and I demand to be returned to my camp," turn to page 84.*

*If you answer, "You are the Grand Canyon," turn to page 90.*

The footsteps wind through the labyrinth until at last you see open space at the end of the passage.

The sight as you emerge from the labyrinth is breathtaking. Horses of all sizes and colors frolic in a lush meadow beside a brook. You never thought any place in the Grand Canyon could be as green as this. The horses from Bill Wilton's ranch are here, as are smaller horses, half the size of normal ones. They are slim and sleek with long legs. They must be the Little Horses.

But what happened to the footsteps and yellow eyes? Ahead of you, watching the horses, is an animal with silver fur, sitting on its haunches. The animal turns and walks over to you.

"If you want to know who has led you here, I will tell you," he says. "Some call me Coyote. I know what you are looking for. The horses have come here to join their long-lost ancestors, the Little Horses. They are happy here."

"Yes, I can see they are happy," you say. But you wonder what you should do. You were sent down the river to bring back Bill's horses. Yet it doesn't seem right to take them away from here.

*If you leave the horses, turn to page 73.*

*If you try to take them back, turn to page 94.*

Suddenly you know you are being watched. A group of bronze-skinned Indians materializes on the trail in front of you. "Greetings," one says.

"Ignore them," Don Pizarro says. "They know nothing."

"My name is Tu-ba," she continues. "We offer you the hospitality of our village."

Don Pizarro waves them off.

You stop. "But, Don Pizarro, don't you want to eat and drink? I'm starving."

"No, I want nothing from these savages," he replies and marches off.

*If you go with Tu-ba to her village, turn to page 95.*

*If you run to catch up with Don Pizarro, turn to page 88.*

"I'm tired of this game," you say. "Take me out of here right now. I want to go back to my camp."

"Ha!" the gila monster cries. There is an explosion of feathers as he sprouts wings and rises above you as an enormous eagle. He digs his talons into the scruff of your neck and carries you out of the labyrinth.

High over the canyon, in the grip of the eagle, you cry, "Where are you taking me?"

"You may be tired of playing my games," the eagle replies sharply, "but you are an intruder here. You must play by our rules."

He cackles and takes you back to his huge nest. The nest is piled high with the bones of horses and humans, all picked clean. Now you know where some of the horses have gone—and you are next on the menu.

**The End**

You let the footsteps go and turn to look for the owner of the voice. "Who said that?" you ask.

"It's me, dummy. Down here."

You look at the ground. In front of you sits a gila monster, eyes flashing.

"Who are you?" you ask, startled.

"I'll ask the questions around here," retorts the gila monster. "Now that you've gotten yourself lost in this labyrinth, I suppose you need help getting out."

I was following these yellow eyes," you explain, "that became footsteps—"

"Footsteps? I didn't see anything go by here. Your ears must be playing tricks on you."

"Oh, forget it," you say. "How do I get out of here?"

"Now hold on just a minute. It's not so easy as that. I'll get you out of here, but only if you can answer my riddle."

"And what if I don't?"

"Then I will decide what to do with you."

"I'll try to answer your riddle," you say. "But after you get me out of here, I have a question for *you.*"

The gila monster nods in agreement, then says, "Are you ready for the riddle?"

"Yes."

"Though I have a mouth, I cannot speak. What am I?"

"That's easy," you say.

---

*If you say, "You are a cave," turn to page 80.*

*If you say, "You are a river," turn to page 79.*

You turn and run toward the scream. You regret leaving the footsteps, but perhaps you can find your way back to them.

The echo of the scream intensifies as you follow it through the labyrinth. Finally you arrive at a pit at the intersection of several passageways. The scream coming from inside it is unearthly and horrible, yet you are drawn to the edge.

You look down and see only darkness. You toss a rock, but you don't hear it hit bottom. Instead, the scream gets louder. You clap your hands over your ears, trying to keep the sound out. But it fills your head. You feel possessed by it. Slowly you fall over the edge of the pit into the darkness. Your fall never stops, and your scream becomes part of the scream of the pit.

**The End**

Don Pizarro is still muttering about the Indians when you join him. "But you'll see," he says. "Soon we will be rich beyond all imagining."

You march on for the rest of the day. Just when you are about to give up hope and tell Don Pizarro he will have to go on without you, he announces, "It is over the next ridge. I can feel it." You wearily decide to follow him to the top of this one last ridge.

When you reach the top, you can hardly believe your eyes. Gleaming towers of diamonds and gold lay on the plain below you. It is a sparkling city of riches, just as Don Pizarro described it.

"Eureka!" Don Pizarro cries, "I've found it! One of the Seven Golden Cities of Cibola!" He runs down the hill toward the city. Dumbfounded, you follow.

When you reach the gates of the city, Don Pizarro is waiting for you with his sword drawn and his feet braced for combat. "It is all mine!" he declares. "If you value your life, you will not enter!"

*If you challenge Don Pizarro, turn to page 70.*

*If you decide to leave the city to him and try to find a way to return to your own time, turn to page 46.*

"You are the Grand Canyon," you answer.

"Right!" the gila monster says. "Now I will tell you how to get out of here. There is a secret rock panel behind me. If you push it, it will open onto the place where you are camped."

"Will you answer my question?" you ask, hoping you aren't pushing your luck.

"It depends on what it is."

"Where are the horses?" you ask.

"The horses! The horses have gone to a pasture in the canyon. Believe me, you will never find them," the gila monster answers and runs off into the labyrinth. You push the panel and walk into camp feeling dazed.

**The End**

You are terrified. It's as if the eyes have deserted you or led you into a trap. You turn and run. You want to get back to the safety of the campfire as fast as possible.

As you race through the darkness, you trip on a rock. You brace yourself for the fall, but the ground isn't beneath you. You fall through the air in the darkness, and you can't see anything below.

With a splash you land in the river.

*Turn to page 18.*

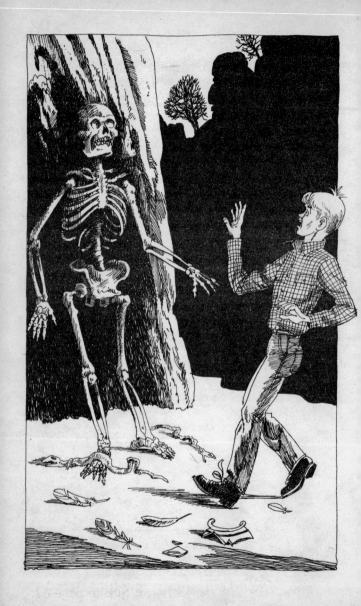

You hesitate for a moment, then continue after the footsteps. The voice didn't sound very friendly.

You follow the sound of the footsteps as they wind through the labyrinth, but their owner is still just out of your sight. Strange things appear on the ground before you. There are brightly colored feathers, freshly shed rattlesnake skins, and broken bits of pottery. Then, coming around a corner, you are stopped by a grisly sight. It is a human skeleton, leaning against the rock wall, one hand outstretched. Suddenly a scream rings out and echoes through the labyrinth. The hairs on the back of your neck stand up. Could the scream be coming from someone in need of help?

*If you follow the echo of the scream,
turn to page 87.*

*If you stick with the footsteps, turn to page 81.*

"The horses belong to Bill Wilton," you say to Coyote. "I must take them back."

"You are making a mistake," Coyote says, "but I cannot stop you."

You try to round the horses up, but they will not obey you. It's obvious they don't want to leave. Yet you persist, and they become angry. One kicks at you, while others paw at the ground.

When you run after a stray, you suddenly hear the roar of hoofbeats behind you. You turn to face a herd of angry stampeding horses! There is little left of you afterward.

**The End**

"Goodbye, Don Pizarro," you call. "I'm staying with Tu-ba. I need something to eat."

Don Pizarro doesn't look back.

Tu-ba takes you to her village. It is cool inside the mud houses. You have a meal of corn and beans, which tastes good. The Indians watch politely while you eat; they wait until you are finished to ask questions. "Where are you going?" Tu-ba asks.

You sigh. "I don't think I can get to where I was going anymore. I'm lost—in a big way. But Don Pizarro is going to the Seven Golden Cities of Cibola. Do you know where they are?"

Tu-ba laughs. "They do not exist. They are a story we made up long ago. We tell it to the Men-Who-Wear-Metal so they will leave us alone."

You laugh, too. "Poor Don Pizarro." Then you think of Delia. "I hope Delia can make it the rest of the way down the river," you say to yourself.

Tu-ba watches you for a while, then says, "Since you seem to be lost, why don't you stay here with us?"

You accept her offer and spend the rest of your days happily raising corn and beans with the Pueblo Indians on the banks of the Colorado.

**The End**

"You'd better send in the helicopter," you tell the ranger. "I don't think we can make it out in the raft."

"Okay," he says. "Give us your position. We'll pick you up tonight."

You tell the ranger your coordinates. "We'll light a fire so you can see us."

You gather a big pile of dry brush and wood, light a bonfire, and settle down to wait for the helicopter. A storm with high winds comes up and pelts you with huge raindrops. "It's going to be pretty hairy for the helicopter in this storm," Delia says.

Soon you hear the chopping of the helicopter's blades overhead. A rope ladder drops down. Delia grabs it and starts climbing. The helicopter swings wildly in the storm, and you know the pilot is having a hard time holding his position. One strong gust and the copter will be smashed against the canyon wall.

You follow Delia. The wind and rain lash you, but you cling to the rope ladder and think only about taking one step at a time. When you make it to the top, the pilot immediately lifts the helicopter out the narrow canyon, just before a strong gust hits.

You are taken back to park headquarters where you can wait for the flood waters to recede and then try again.

**The End**

"Thank you for your offer," you say to Don Pizarro. "But I cannot join you. I have my own search."

Don Pizarro looks hurt, then boils up into a red rage. He draws his sword and holds the point at your chest. "No one refuses Don Pizarro!" he cries. "If you will not join me as my partner, you will join me as my slave!" Then he becomes suspicious. "Or perhaps you really do know where the Seven Golden Cities of Cibola are, and you want them all to yourself? Greedy ingrate! No one holds out on Don Pizarro!"

"Don Pizarro," you say calmly. "Listen to me. I've never even heard of the Seven Golden Cities."

"I know a gold hunter when I see one," he replies and ties a rope around your neck. "You will be my slave."

All day he leads you through canyons and over ridges in his search for the cities. You feel like a dog on a leash. Near the end of the day you finally stumble onto a high plateau.

"Stop!" a voice commands from the bushes. Don Pizarro stops, and soon a group of Pueblo Indians appears. "I am Palata," one says. "Who are you?"

"I am Signor Don Pizarro de Manquila," Don Pizarro announces.

The Indians look at you curiously. "And who is this person on the rope?"

"My slave," Don Pizarro explains.

*Turn to page 111.*

"I have to get back to my world," you insist.

"It is very dangerous," Wapa-tayu warns. "You will be attempting to travel from one dimension to another."

"But I must try," you say.

"Very well, then," she says, sighing. "I will do my best to help you. I'll try to return you to your dimension. Close your eyes," she commands. You close them. She stands over you and chants a song of return. She invokes the seven directions, and suddenly you feel yourself spinning through the air. An enormous thunderclap sounds in your ears, then there is silence.

You open your eyes and see the blue-green earth hovering below you. Huge chunks of the earth's crust are being uplifted into mountain ranges, then worn down again. Oceans swell and recede, and rivers carve out gigantic canyons. Volcanoes erupt and masses of molten lava pour out. You can't tell which is moving, you or the things in front of you, but you realize you are seeing nothing less than the creation of the earth—in reverse!

*If you cry, "Stop!" turn to page 103.*

*If you let yourself keep going,
turn to page 112.*

You dive down as far as you can go. After you hit bottom, you push back up for air. But when your head breaks the surface, the air sears your lungs. You dive back into the water. You know you don't want to go up again.

As you swim under the water, you realize you are having no trouble breathing. You don't need air. Then you realize you have no arms or legs and that you are swimming with fins. You look over and recognize a fish swimming next to you—Delia! Now you understand what has happened. You have become a fish in the Great Flood. At least you know to watch out for worms on hooks.

**The End**

"Don Pizarro is my partner and an honorable man," you say.

"Very well," says Palata. "Then I will take you both to the Seven Golden Cities."

Don Pizarro can hardly contain himself as Palata leads you both across the plateau to the edge of a cliff. A thousand feet below you can see the river. It looks tiny from that height.

"The golden cities are between here and the river," Palata says. Don Pizarro leans out to look and Palata gives him a hearty shove over the edge. His screams fade as he falls. Then Palata turns to you and explains, "We don't like greedy intruders. Now it is your turn!"

## The End

You think for a while and decide you would like to learn Wapa-tayu's ways. "I'll stay with you," you tell her.

"Good," she says. "You will not regret it. The only thing required is patience. We will teach you how to exist out of time."

Wapa-tayu is true to her word, and soon you are learning to see beyond time.

**The End**

Your cry of "Stop!" rings in your ears. You feel your movement slow, then finally stop. You are frozen at the moment when the earth is a newly forming ball of molten rock. The heat of the swirling liquid rock begins to close in on you. Slowly you feel yourself melt and dissolve into the boiling mass.

Hundreds of centuries later you will reappear, embedded in the walls of the Grand Canyon.

## The End

You try to relax, keeping your head above water and drifting with the current. Exhausted from staying up all night, you feel dizzy as the cold water carries you along. You close your eyes for a moment. . . .

When you open them, you jump. You are not in the water, but on a straw bed. As your eyes adjust to the half-light, you see you are in a small square room with a dirt floor and mud walls. Three figures are moving slowly into the room, swaying to a rhythm you can't hear. Their bodies are painted in brightly colored symbols, and they have ruffs of spruce around their necks. One wears an enormous wooden bird beak filled with teeth on his head, another a buffalo head decorated with symbols of lightning, and the third a deer head hung with eagle feathers.

They chant a slow dirge and rattle gourds as they dance around you. They are singing a welcoming song for you—as if you were dead!

*If you flee the room, turn to page 115.*

*If you wait for a chance to ask what is going on, go on to the next page.*

You wait for a pause in the chanting, then sit up and ask, "Where am I?"

The three dancers stop abruptly and stare at you. They retreat to the other side of the room.

"Where am I?" you repeat.

They cautiously approach. One reaches out a hand and touches you. "Are you—alive?" he asks.

"I *think* so," you say.

He looks at the others. "We'd better find Wapa-tayu. She will know what to do."

They disappear out the door and soon return with an old woman who has long white hair and a maze of wrinkles on her face. "I am Wapa-tayu, the medicine woman," she says, peering at you. "Where do you come from?"

"I was on a raft trip with my friend Delia, and we got caught in a flood. Who are you?"

"You might know us as the Anasazi—the Ancient Ones."

"Then—I've traveled through time?" you ask slowly.

*Go on to the next page.*

"In a way," she answers. "But we do not really exist in time. This is the place our people come to after they leave your world."

"How can I get back to my own time?" you ask.

Wapa-tayu wrinkles her brow. "I do not think that is possible. If you tried to return, I am afraid you would get caught between our dimension and yours. We exist out of time, as I said. I do not know why you would want to go back, anyway. Our prophecies foresee doom for your world."

*If you demand to know what she means by existing out of time, turn to page 110.*

*If you ask about the prophecies, go on to the next page.*

# 108

"What are the prophecies?" you ask Wapa-tayu.

"They are very grim," she says, shaking her head. "The world is destroyed by fire. It lies burned for a long time. It is very sad. But, after a long while, good comes of it. The spirits of our dimension—the world out of time—will return to the earth, as will all previous life forms; and the gods will remove their masks."

You are speechless. It is a frightening picture. Finally you say, "Can you tell me how to survive the destruction? Perhaps I can go back to my world and find shelter from the flames."

She shakes her head. "There is no shelter from evil. Stay here with us. Our world is not out of balance like yours. You can come with us when we return to the earth."

"But I can't just abandon Delia and the horses," you say.

"Don't worry about them," Wapa-tayu says. "There are more important things. Stay with us."

*If you decide to stay with the Anasazi,
turn to page 102.*

*If you insist you must try to get back to your
own world, turn to page 99.*

"Don Pizarro is a tyrant who cares only for gold," you say. "He is not to be trusted."

Palata nods. "I thought so. We will send him off to find the Seven Golden Cities by himself." Palata removes the rope from your neck, and his warriors run screaming at Don Pizarro. He cringes and flees across the plateau into the distance.

"Now," Palata says, "would you join us for a meal in our village?"

You accept his offer. After dinner you summon the courage to tell Palata your story and ask for help. "I'm from the future," you tell him. "But somehow the river has brought me back to this time. I was on a raft trip, looking for some lost horses. Now I'm not sure what to do."

*Turn to page 113.*

"What do you mean you exist out of time?" you demand.

"I simply mean we exist in the dimension above and beyond time—and beyond your world," Wapa-tayu explains. "Time spreads before us as you might spread a map. But it is not easy to read. It requires much practice."

You are impatient. You want to get back to your own time. Wapa-tayu studies you for a while, then says, "I think you must have come here by mistake. You do not seem to belong."

"You're telling me!" you say. "I want to leave."

"You are free to do as you please," Wapa-tayu says.

"Then goodbye," you say as you leave the room. You are glad to get away from Wapa-tayu and her strange talk.

You decide to return to the river. The water flows fast and clear. You hesitate for a moment, then dive in.

*Turn to page 100.*

The Indians withdraw to confer among themselves. Palata calls to Don Pizarro, "Are you in search of the great cities of gold?"

"Yes," he answers excitedly. "Where are they?"

Palata motions you over and asks in a low voice, "Tell me first, Person-on-the-Rope, is this Don Pizarro an honorable man? Why does he enslave you? We have seen the Men-Who-Wear-Metal before. Are they worthy of the golden cities?"

You have to decide what to answer. This may be your chance to be free of Don Pizarro once and for all. On the other hand, if the cities of Cibola really do exist, you may not see them if you denounce Don Pizarro.

*If you say, "Don Pizarro is a tyrant who cares only for gold," turn to page 109.*

*If you say, "Don Pizarro is my partner and an honorable man," turn to page 101.*

Fascinated, you watch the molten earth dissolve before you. You are floating out beyond the earth in the vast universe. Suddenly you feel very alone.

"Wapa-tayu!" you cry. "Help me!"

But it is too late. The sun appears and implodes in a massive hydrogen explosion. Galaxies form and disperse in spectacular wheeling shapes. Faster and faster, approaching the speed of light, you go all the way back to the first moment. The universe is born in a tremendous explosion.

You are vaporized and reborn as billions of separate quarks.

**The End**

Palata thinks for a long while. "I have heard many stories of time travel but know nothing for sure. Tonight we can show you a magical spot to sleep. We will sprinkle antler dust on you—then perhaps the night winds will come and take you back to your own time.

"As for the horses, I can give you some good advice. There are many things we know about the canyon from living here over the centuries, and one of them is that there is a place in the canyon that horses are drawn to. I can tell you how to get there, and if your time is not completely different from ours, you may find them there."

You sleep in the place Palata shows you that night. In the morning you find yourself back in your own time with Delia. You go to the spot in the canyon Palata told you about, and the horses are there, just as he predicted.

**The End**

You stay, admiring the glitter of the golden city. You and Don Pizarro are probably the richest people on earth. But as the years go by, your fascination with gold wears off. You have nowhere to spend it. You understand why the Pueblo Indians have ignored the city. In your later years, you become bitter. All this gold has done you no good—you've had no one to share it with. You wonder what happened to your friend Delia. . . .

**The End**

This is too weird, you think to yourself as you dash out of the room.

You find yourself in a honeycombed cliff dwelling. You clamber down through the rooms and out into the canyon, hoping to find the river. You're not sure what you'll do when you get there, but it is your only point of reference.

Your sense of direction is gone, though, and it takes you two days of wandering to realize you are hopelessly lost. In your last moments, before you succumb to the hot sun, you think you have found a lake of clear blue water. But there is only sand under your feet.

**The End**

## ABOUT THE AUTHOR

JAY LEIBOLD was born in Denver, Colorado, and now lives in San Francisco, California. His first Choose Your Own Adventure book was *Sabotage*. This is his second, and he has completed a third, which is set during the American Revolution.

## ABOUT THE ILLUSTRATOR

DON HEDIN was the first artist for the Choose Your Own Adventure series, working under the name of Paul Granger, and has illustrated over twenty-five books for the series. For many years, Mr. Hedin was associated with *Reader's Digest* as a staff illustrator and then art editor. With his wife, who is also an artist, Mr. Hedin now lives in Oak Creek Canyon, Arizona, where he continues to work as a fine-arts painter and illustrator.

# CHOOSE YOUR OWN ADVENTURE ®

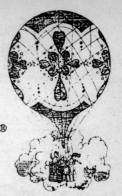

"You'll want all the books in the exciting Choose Your Own Adventure series. Each book takes you through dozens of fantasy adventures—under the sea, in a space colony, into the past—in which *you* are the main character. What happens next in the story depends on the choices *you* make, and *only you* can decide how the story ends!"

## Make sure you have all these great Interplanetary Spy books!

| | | | |
|---|---|---|---|
| ☐ | 23506 | **Find The Kirillian! #1**<br>McEvoy, Hempel & Wheatley | $1.95 |
| ☐ | 23507 | **The Galactic Pirate #2**<br>McEvoy, Hempel & Wheatley | $1.95 |
| ☐ | 23700 | **Robot World #3**<br>McEvoy, Hempel & Wheatley | $1.95 |
| ☐ | 23701 | **Space Olympics #4**<br>Martinez and Pierard | $1.95 |
| ☐ | 23941 | **Monsters of Doorna #5**<br>McEvoy, Hempel & Wheatley | $1.95 |
| ☐ | 23942 | **The Star Crystal #6**<br>R. Martinez and R. Larson | $1.95 |
| ☐ | 24198 | **Rebel Spy #7**  L. Neufeld | $1.95 |
| ☐ | 24521 | **Mission to Microworld #8**  S. McEvoy | $1.95 |
| ☐ | 24425 | **Ultraheroes #9**  L. Neufeld & M. Banks | $1.95 |
| ☐ | 24532 | **Planet Hunters #10**   Seth McEvoy | $1.95 |

**Prices and availability subject to change without notice.**

Buy these exciting Interplanetary Spy adventures wherever Bantam paperbacks are sold, or use this handy coupon for ordering:

---

Bantam Books, Inc., Dept. INS, 414 East Golf Road, Des Plaines, Ill. 60016

Please send me the books I have checked above. I am enclosing $_____
(please add $1.25 to cover postage and handling). Send check or money order
—no cash or C.O.D.'s please.

Mr/Mrs/Miss _____

Address_____

City_____ State/Zip_____

INS—3/85

Please allow four to six weeks for delivery. This offer expires 9/85.

# SPECIAL
# MONEY SAVING
# OFFER

Now you can have an up-to-date listing of Bantam's hundreds of titles plus take advantage of our unique and exciting bonus book offer. A special offer which gives you the opportunity to purchase a Bantam book for only 50¢. Here's how!

By ordering any five books at the regular price per order, you can also choose any other single book listed (up to a $4.95 value) for just 50¢. Some restrictions do apply, but for further details why not send for Bantam's listing of titles today!

Just send us your name and address plus 50¢ to defray the postage and handling costs.

# BLAST INTO THE PAST!

## TIME MACHINE

Each of these books is a time machine and you are at the controls . . .

- ☐ 23601   **SECRETS OF THE KNIGHTS #1**   $1.95
  J. Gasperini

- ☐ 23502   **SEARCH FOR DINOSAURS #2**   $1.95
  D. Bischoff

- ☐ 24052   **SWORD OF THE SAMURAI #3**   $1.95
  M. Reaves & S. Perry

- ☐ 23808   **SAIL WITH PIRATES #4**   $1.95
  J. Gasperini

- ☐ 24183   **CIVIL WAR SECRET AGENT #5**   $1.95
  Steve Perry

- ☐ 24424   **THE RINGS OF SATURN #6**   $1.95
  Arthur Cover

**Prices and availability subject to change without notice.**

---

**Buy them at your local bookstore or use this handy coupon for ordering:**